This book belongs to:

Bearific's® Fashion Adventure

Written & Illustrated by:
Katelyn Lonas

It was a glorious day in Berrytown.

1

Berra Mall

I'm looking for new clothes at Berra Mall.

$79.99

All the clothes were extravagant and out of my price range.

Now I need to find
a way to make
more money.

I dialed Charm's number then I asked if she wanted to start a business together to make money.

We agreed to meet at Berra Cafe.

Charm and I ordered
tropical juice.

We began
brainstorming ideas
for a business.

Finally we agreed to start a
fashion business.

We headed back to
my house.

We were thinking of names and unique fashion designs.

Berra Craft Store

Charm and I flew to Berra
Craft Store.

We bought some
colorful fabrics
and supplies.

13

We paid for everything and we hurried back to my house.

Charm began sewing the clothes.

I made the accessories and
jewelry.

After weeks of exhaustion and hard work, we finished!

17

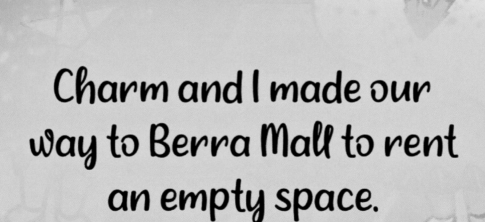

Charm and I made our
way to Berra Mall to rent
an empty space.

The next day, we moved in all our products.

We finished setting everything up in our store.

The next step was
to hire some
employees.

Finally our store was
ready to open!

On opening day not
even a single bear
fairy came in to our
store.

Promote

Charm and I realized we had to promote and advertise our store.

We decided to have a fashion show while wearing our unique clothes.

25

Fashion Show

Collections from Bearific & Charm's Fashion Store

Date:
Saturday, 5/30

Time:
6:30pm

Location:
Bearific & Charm's Fashion Store

Charm and I started making flyers for our fashion show.

We called
some of our
friends to see if
they would like
to model in our
fashion show.

Charm and I passed out our flyers to everyone in Berrytown.

We went to Berra Local
Store to buy things for
our fashion show.

Later we finished setting up our fashion show.

Our friends were
getting ready to walk
down the run way.

31

Bearific & Charm's

Fashion Show

There were so many bear fairies at our fashion show!

Once our fashion show was over, we cleaned up everything.

33

Bearific & Charm's Fashion Store

Grand Opening

Grand Opening

The next day we went to open our store and there was a line of bear fairies waiting to get in!

Our store was packed
with bear fairies for the
rest of the day!

At the end of the
day, we sold out of
everything!

36

Bearific & Charm's Fashion Store

Grand Open... Grand Opening

Now our fashion store
was quite the adventure!

The End!

Fun Facts

- Close to 2 billion t-shirts are sold every year.
- The first fashion magazine was sold in Germany during 1586.
- Charles Frederick Worth is known as the father of fashion.

DIY: No Sew Pillow

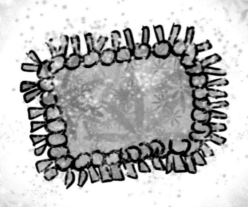

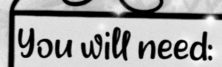

You will need:
- fabric
- scissors
- stuffing

1. Cut two equal pieces of fabric to your desired size.

2.

Cut a square off each corner (just like the drawing). Make sure you do it exactly the same to both pieces of the fabric.

3.

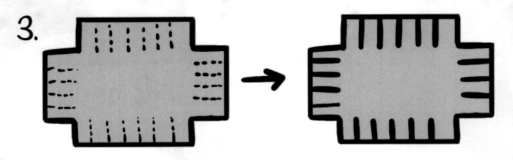

Cut lines along each side of the fabric (just like the drawing). Make sure to do it exactly the same to both pieces of the fabric. Don't cut past where the square ends.

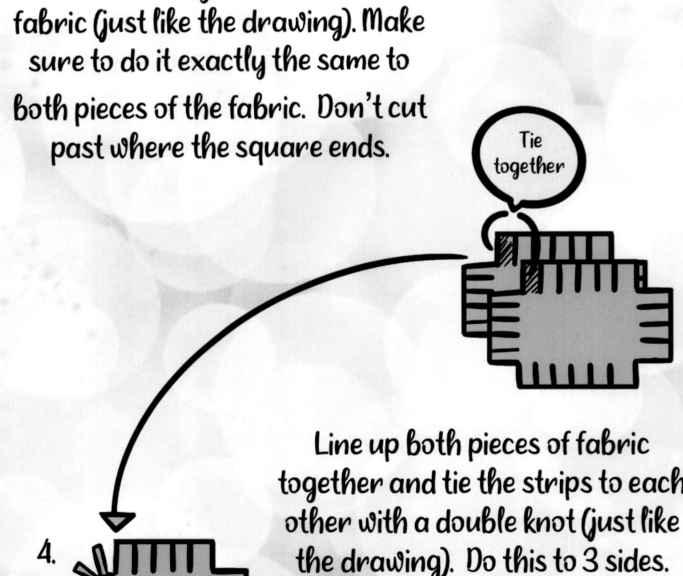

Tie together

Line up both pieces of fabric together and tie the strips to each other with a double knot (just like the drawing). Do this to 3 sides.

4.

5.

Take your stuffing and fill it in your pillow.

After you filled it with stuffing
finish tying your pillow.

6.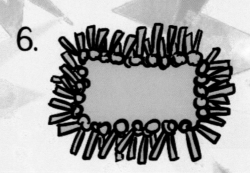

7.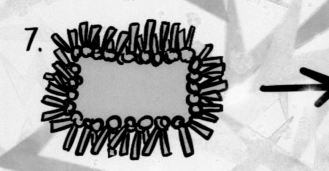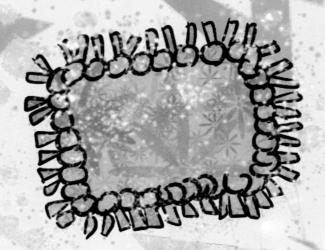

Now decorate and add designs to your pillow!
You are finished!

FASHION
word search

```
qwertyuiopasrefts
bearifichwitrcharm
hdhdiejcneisjsewuhi
kmfjnestorefheunfj
fashiondheudebef
clothesshwdhfgh
ffwqejifjewelryry
rghgfdqwertyuiop
```

•Bearific • Charm • fashion • store •

clothes • jewelry • sew•

remember to:

BELIEVE

DREAM

ACHIEVE

Read my other books:

More adventures are coming soon!

Katelyn Lonas

Katelyn is a 13 year old who resides in Southern California. She started writing and illustrating her first book at age 9 and then published 6 more books. She hopes you enjoy this book and had fun making a no sew pillow. Thank you for reading Bearific's® Fashion Adventure and be ready for more adventures to come!

— Katelyn

Made in the USA
Columbia, SC
03 July 2021